Uncle '
Pirate Adventure

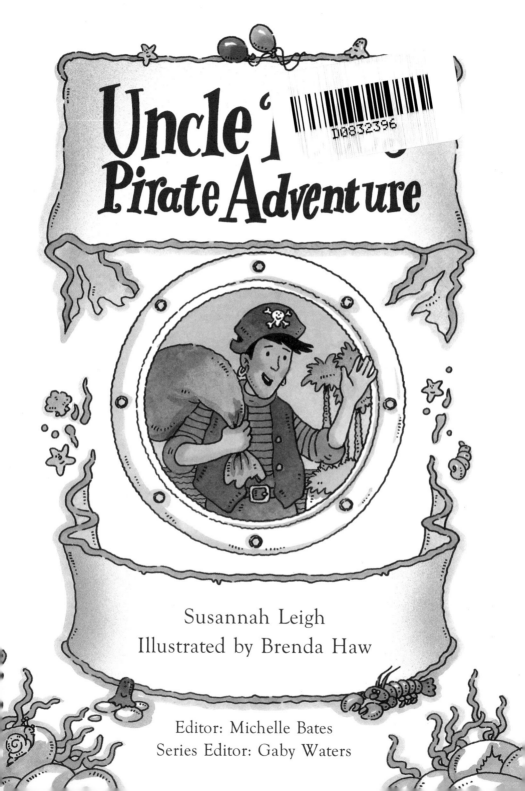

Susannah Leigh

Illustrated by Brenda Haw

Editor: Michelle Bates
Series Editor: Gaby Waters

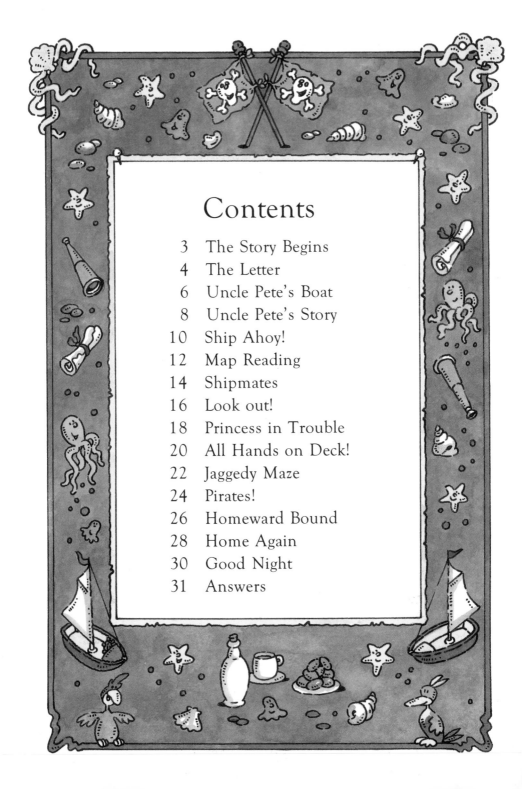

Contents

3   The Story Begins
4   The Letter
6   Uncle Pete's Boat
8   Uncle Pete's Story
10 Ship Ahoy!
12 Map Reading
14 Shipmates
16 Look out!
18 Princess in Trouble
20 All Hands on Deck!
22 Jaggedy Maze
24 Pirates!
26 Homeward Bound
28 Home Again
30 Good Night
31 Answers

The Story Begins

One day Mary was playing with her friend Zac. They were pretending to be pirates. Suddenly they heard a knock at the door. Mary ran to open it, but no one was there. On the doorstep was a letter. Turn the page to find out what the letter said...

This story is full of puzzles to solve.

If you get stuck there are answers on pages 31 and 32.

The Letter

Dear 👧 and 👦
I need your help.
Come to the 🚢
and look
for a ⛵ like this.
I will be on board.
Don't forget to ask Mary's
first!
❤ from 🏴‍☠️

"This letter is from my Uncle Pete," Mary said. "He's a pirate and he needs our help. Come on Zac, let's go and find him!"

Have you read the letter? Where are they going?

5

Uncle Pete's Boat

Mary and Zac raced down to the sea to find Uncle Pete's boat, but which one was it? It wasn't going to be easy to find. There were lots of boats! Big boats and small boats, old boats and new boats.

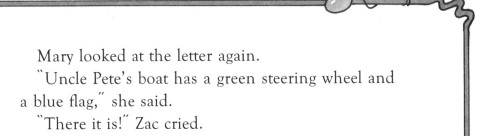

Mary looked at the letter again.

"Uncle Pete's boat has a green steering wheel and a blue flag," she said.

"There it is!" Zac cried.

Can you see Uncle Pete's boat?

7

Uncle Pete's Story

Uncle Pete gave Mary a big hug. He gave Zac a pirate handshake. He was very pleased to see them.

"Welcome aboard me hearties," he cried. "I'm glad you've come. I need your help."

Mary and Zac climbed onto the little pirate boat and sat down.

"What's the problem, Uncle Pete?" Mary asked.

"I've lost my pirate pals," Uncle Pete replied. "Listen very carefully and I'll tell you how it happened..."

We were at sea when there was a fierce storm. My pirate pals fell overboard. They swam to a nearby island. I managed to stay on the boat.

The storm finished, but I had drifted miles from the island.

At last I reached home, where I mended my damaged boat.

"You didn't quite finish mending your boat, Uncle Pete!" Mary and Zac cried together. "Look!"

Can you see what Mary and Zac have spotted?

9

Ship Ahoy!

Uncle Pete put an enormous piece of pirate sticking tape over the hole.

"Well spotted," he said. "Now listen carefully. I must go back to the island and rescue my pirate pals. But it takes at least three people to sail my boat. One to steer, one to read the map and one to keep lookout. You will help, won't you?"

"Of course we will," cried Mary and Zac.

"Then let's set sail!" said Uncle Pete. "I'll take the wheel. Zac, you climb to the top of the crow's-nest and keep a lookout. Mary, you read the map. There are lots of boats to sail around before we can reach the open sea. It's tricky, but we can do it, me hearties!"

Can you find a way between the boats and out to the open sea?

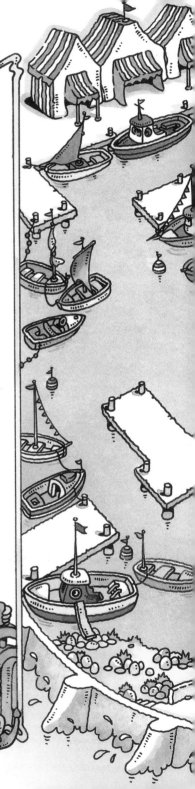

11

Map Reading

At last they were on their way. Mary spread the map out in front of her.

"Which island did your pirate pals swim to, Uncle Pete?" she asked.

"Oh dear," Uncle Pete replied. "I can't remember its name." He thought hard.

Double Trouble Island

Rock Island

Spooky Isle

Barrel of Laughs Island

Monkey Island

Rumbling Tum Island

"I'm sure it had a volcano. I know we passed some dolphins just before the storm broke. And I had to sail around some jaggedy rocks nearby. There were red jellyfish in the water too!

Mary looked at the map closely. "Then there's only one island it could possibly be, Uncle Pete!" she said.

Which island is it?

Uncle Pete's map of the Islands
(not to scale)

Firecracker Island

Flagpole Island

Pancake Island

Prickly Pea Island

Tall Trees Island

13

Shipmates

Uncle Pete turned the boat toward Prickly Pea Island and they sailed on.

"What are your pirate pals like, Uncle Pete?" Zac called.

"Come down and I'll tell you all about them," said Uncle Pete. "Their names are Dave Doubloon, Betty Buccaneer and Lester Lagoon."

Dave Doubloon is the navigator. He reads the map and tells me which way to sail.

Betty Buccaneer is second in command. If I've got scurvy or feel seasick, Betty takes charge.

Lester Lagoon is the lookout man. He wears a head scarf.

My pirate pals

"Lester has an eye patch too! And Betty has a pet parrot," Zac cried. "Why yes," said Uncle Pete in surprise. "But how did you know?"

How does Zac know what Uncle Pete's pirate pals look like?

Look out!

Zac scrambled back up the crow's-nest to do some more looking out.

"Everything looks very busy from up here, Uncle Pete," he called.

Zac looked out to sea again. But this time, things were different and someone was in trouble!

Can you spot the differences? Who is in trouble?

Princess in Trouble

Uncle Pete pulled out his special shark-scaring whistle, just in time. PEEP! The sharks swam away quickly.

"Well spotted Zac," said Uncle Pete.

Then a big boat sailed up beside them.

"Uncle Pete," called the captain. "This is the royal boat and the princess is on board, but all of her jewels have gone! Can you help us?"

Boo hoo!

18

"Don't worry," said Uncle Pete. "Pirates are good at finding precious jewels. What has she lost?"

"A gold, sparkly necklace, a beautiful red bracelet and a twinkly golden crown," said the captain. "I hope they haven't fallen overboard."

"It's all right, Uncle Pete," Mary cried. "The jewels are still on board the ship. Look!"

Can you find the princess's jewels?

All Hands on Deck!

The princess gave a regal wave as her ship sailed away. Suddenly there was a shout from behind. Uncle Pete, Mary and Zac spun around to see a steamboat puffing up behind them.

"Swashbuckling sword fights!" cried Uncle Pete. "Bad Luck Bill is on board that boat!"

Mary shivered. "Bad Luck Bill. Who's he?"

"He's the meanest pirate on the high seas," Uncle Pete cried.

"Watch out," cried Mary. "He's heading this way."

"Yikes," said Zac.

With a mighty leap, Bad Luck Bill landed on board Uncle Pete's boat. He shook his fist and brandished his cutlass.

Mary shivered. They were in trouble now. But Zac had spotted something.

"Bad Luck Bill's the one in trouble, Mary," he whispered.

What has Zac spotted?

Ha ha! Give me all your treasure, Uncle Pete. You're bound to have some.

Jaggedy Maze

The octopus curled its tentacle around Bad Luck Bill's ankle and pulled sharply. SPLASH! Bad Luck Bill landed in the water. "I'll get you next time, Uncle Pete," he gurgled.

Mary looked at the map again. "We're very near the island now, Uncle Pete," she said. Suddenly, Zac gave a shout.

"Prickly Pea Island is straight ahead," he called.

"But watch out for the jaggedy rocks," warned Mary. "There are lots more here than on your map, Uncle Pete. You'll have to steer very carefully."

Can you help Uncle Pete find a way through the jaggedy rocks to the island?

23

Pirates!

Carefully, Uncle Pete steered the little boat through the maze of jaggedy rocks. Here it was. Prickly Pea Island at last! They dropped anchor and jumped ashore.

"Hmm," said Uncle Pete. "It's quiet on this island. Too quiet. Where are my pirate pals? Have they been rescued already?"

"Perhaps they're hiding," said Mary. "Just in case we aren't friendly pirates."

They looked high and low.

"Aha!" Zac cried at last. "I think I can see them."

Can you spot Dave Doubloon, Lester Lagoon and Betty Buccaneer?

Homeward Bound

Uncle Pete gave his pirate pals a big hug. Then
everyone clambered back on board the boat. Uncle
Pete pulled up the anchor and then they were off.

"Goodbye Prickly Pea Island!" called Lester
Lagoon. "We won't be back."

"Homeward bound!" cried Dave Doubloon.

"Shiver me timbers, Uncle Pete!" said Betty
Buccaneer, "We're starving. Any ship's biscuits
on board?"

"I can do better than that," Uncle Pete replied with a twinkle in his eye. "There's green Jolly Roger dessert, swashbuckling sandwiches and chocolate cake as well. There's landlubbers lemonade and pirate pop to drink. But where did I put everything?"

"We'll find it," Mary and Zac cried as the pirate friends sat down to eat.

Can you help find the pirate feast?

Home Again

When they arrived back, Mary said, "Come and play at my house."

"Sorry," said Lester Lagoon. "I have to bake a cake."

"My cat needs feeding," said Betty Buccaneer.

"And I've got to mend my bike," said Dave Doubloon.

"I'll come," said Uncle Pete.

"Me too!" said Zac.

And so they did...

Uncle Pete, Mary and Zac went home.
Mary's mother said, "Come and have some cherry
cake and tell me all about your day."

"Yum. Yes please," cried Mary and Zac. "Being a pirate
is hungry work."

As they were munching their cake, there was a knock at
the door. It was Zac's parents.

It's time to come home, Zac!

Good Night!

Soon it was Mary's bedtime. Uncle Pete tucked her in
and read her a bedtime story about boats and islands
and pirates and treasure.

"That was a good story, Uncle Pete," Mary sighed.
"But not as good as the pirate adventure we had
today. Good night."

"Good night Mary," said her parents.

"Good night Mary," said Uncle Pete, with a smile.

Answers

Pages 4-5

You shouldn't have trouble reading this letter. Just replace the pictures with their words.

Mary and Zac are going to look for Uncle Pete's boat.

Pages 6-7

Uncle Pete's boat is here.

Pages 8-9

Mary and Zac have spotted a hole in Uncle Pete's boat. Water is gushing through it!

Pages 10-11

The safe way to the open sea is shown in black.

Pages 12-13

Uncle Pete's pals are on Prickly Pea Island. It is the only island that matched Uncle Pete's description.

Pages 14-15

Zac has seen this picture of Uncle Pete's pirate pals.

Pages 16-17

The differences are circled in black. The windsurfer is in trouble.

Pages 18-19

The princess's jewels are circled in black.

Pages 20-21

Zac has spotted an octopus curling its tentacle around Bill's leg.

Pages 22-23

The way trough the jaggedy rocks to the island is shown in black.

Pages 24-25

The six red jellyfish are circled in black.

Here is Dave Doubloon.   Here is Lester Lagoon.   Here is Betty Buccaneer.

Pages 26-27

The food and drink for the pirate feast are circled in black.

Pages 28-29

Did you spot something familiar about Zac's parents?

Page 30

Where have you seen Mary's dad before

This edition first published in 2002 by Usborne Publishing Ltd., Usborne House, 83-85 Saffron Hill, London EC1N 8RT, England. www.usborne.com Copyright © 2002, 1995 Usborne Publishing Ltd. The name Usborne and the devices 🖊 🎈 are Trade Marks of Usborne Publishing Ltd. All rights reserved.